The Friendship Hedge

by Gunilla B. Norris

illustrated by Dale Payson

❧ E. P. DUTTON & CO., INC. NEW YORK ❧

LIBRARY OF CONGRESS CATALOGING IN PUBLICATION DATA

Norris, Gunilla Brodde, 1939–   The friendship hedge.

SUMMARY: Alice's determination to teach her best friend
a lesson about the guinea pig that has come between them
leads to a painful lesson for both girls.

[1. Friendship—Fiction]   I. Payson, Dale, illus.   II. Title.
PZ7.N7916Fr   [Fic]   73-77449
ISBN 0-525-30210-7

Published simultaneously in Canada by Clarke,
Irwin & Company Limited, Toronto and Vancouver

Designed by Riki Levinson
Printed in the U.S.A.
First Edition

For Jennifer, with love

❧ *Chapter One* ❦

Impatiently Alice looked up at the school clock. Two-thirty, almost the end of the day. She glanced over at her best friend, Claire, on the other side of the room. Claire's blond, curly head was bending over her math paper. Alice could see the frown of concentration on Claire's face as she worked, carefully and methodically. Claire never did anything fast.

Alice drummed her long fingers on the desk. It made a muffled, steady noise. Underneath the desk her long legs moved back and forth. Alice had the tallest desk in the room, but even so her feet banged against the floor.

Now Alice could feel Mrs. Crandle looking at her. Alice pretended not to notice. She swung her legs back and forth again and drummed her fingers on the desk.

Mrs. Crandle cleared her throat. "I think I hear a marching band at the back of the room," she said.

Alice blushed. Still, she couldn't stop her legs from going. Why didn't Claire look up? Alice wanted to give her their special signal—the signal to meet by the water fountain.

Albert Stone snickered and Jessica Horton crossed her brown little eyes at Alice. Alice paid no attention. Her eyes were on Claire. And still Claire didn't look up. She was the last one in the room working on her math. Everyone was don. . Alice saw Claire purse her lips and struggle with the numbers. Claire didn't need to be *that* careful, did she? She always made good grades anyhow. Alice frowned.

How could she make Claire look up? Alice chewed on her lip. She darted a look at Mrs. Crandle. Her teacher was busy copying something. Surreptitiously Alice drew out three books from underneath her desk. She propped them close to the edge of the desk top. Another look at Mrs. Crandle. All clear. With her eyes fastened on Claire, Alice gave the books a quick jab. They fell to the floor with a loud bang.

Claire's startled eyes looked up. Alice quickly

gave the water fountain signal, a hand cupped to her mouth. But Claire only frowned and shook her head "no" impatiently.

"Alice?" Mrs. Crandle was coming down the aisle to stand by her desk. "What are you doing?"

"I was just trying to clean up my desk a little," mumbled Alice as she ducked down to pick up the heap of books on the floor.

"That's a noisy way to go about it, isn't it?" said Mrs. Crandle.

"They fell," said Alice lamely.

"With a little help," mumbled Jessica sarcastically from across the aisle.

But Mrs. Crandle didn't hear. "Alice, you seem very restless," she said. "Why don't you collect the math papers?"

"But I'm not finished!" complained Claire, her head coming up from the math paper with a distressed look.

"Hurry along, then, Claire. The bell is going to ring soon," said Mrs. Crandle.

"But I can't," said Claire. Her voice wavered.

"Do your best," said Mrs. Crandle. "Go ahead, Alice, gather up the papers."

Alice stood up. Quickly she moved along the front rows, snatching up papers as she went. She'd only done half the room when the bell rang. All at once the classroom broke up into a hubbub. Suddenly it was hard to gather up the papers. Everyone shoved and got in Alice's way. Jessica held her paper behind her back, out of reach, and smiled at Alice with a big toothy grin. Alice tried to snatch it from her, but Jessica jumped out of the way. Alice went after her and stumbled over her own desk chair, falling down and banging her shin. Then Jessica laughed and slapped the paper down on the desk. When Alice picked herself up, Jessica was almost out the door.

"Slow down, Alice," called Mrs. Crandle above the noise. "Wait till everyone's left."

Alice glowered at Jessica's math paper. She wanted to tear it to bits. But instead she made herself put it in the pile. Now she stood in the aisle and waited, shifting from one foot to the other.

Finally everyone was gone except Claire, who was still working. Alice looked at Mrs. Crandle.

"All right, Alice," Mrs. Crandle nodded.

Fast and furiously Alice gathered up papers. She came to Claire's desk last of all. Without waiting another minute, she grabbed at Claire's paper.

"Alice, don't!" wailed Claire, holding on. "I'm not finished."

"But the bell rang," said Alice firmly, "and I waited to pick yours up last." She gave a quick tug and the next instant the paper ripped in two.

"Alice!" Mrs. Crandle's voice sounded sharp. "What's got into you? It's not polite to snatch someone's paper when they're still working on it."

Claire burst out in tears. "You tore it!" she cried. "Look what you've done. You tore it!"

Alice looked down at the paper. Her face turned pale. "I didn't mean to," she said softly.

"Just because you're so fast!" Claire's face flushed. "Everybody isn't like you."

Mrs. Crandle came over.

"Alice, Alice." She shook her head. "Whatever has got into you? You know better than that. I have a mind to keep you in after school."

"I didn't mean to," murmured Alice. She looked straight into Mrs. Crandle's blue eyes. "I just . . . I just wanted Claire to hurry because we're spending the night together. We always spend one night together on the weekends like . . . like sisters," she said earnestly. She wanted Mrs. Crandle to understand. "And there's lots to plan, Mrs. Crandle, lots."

"But you live right next door to each other!" exclaimed Mrs. Crandle.

"I know. But we haven't decided whether it's Claire's house this weekend or mine, and there's such a lot of stuff to do. . . ."

"Well," Mrs. Crandle frowned and tried not to smile. But she smiled all the same, and Alice wondered if Mrs. Crandle remembered having a best friend too, long ago.

"I *am* sorry," said Alice, apologizing again. "If I scotch tape it, the paper will be good as new," she said confidently. "Won't it, Claire?"

Claire shook her head, but Alice didn't notice. She'd already run for the tape and was busy mending the torn paper.

"There! Better than new," announced Alice, and she put the paper on top of all the others.

"But I didn't finish," said Claire. Her tear-stained face was still flushed.

"All the same," said Mrs. Crandle, patting Claire on the back, "it's time to stop. I'm sure you've done a good job. You always do. Run along, girls, and have a nice weekend."

Alice flashed her a bright smile. "Thank you, Mrs. Crandle, we will," she called gaily over her shoulder and ran ahead out the door.

But Claire didn't say anything. For a minute she stared after Alice, and then slowly she followed, moving along one step at a time.

❧ *Chapter Two* ❦

Her packing was almost done. Alice looked around her room for the last few things to put in her overnight bag.

"Mom," she called, "where's my red nightgown?"

"Isn't it in your drawer?" Her mother came into the room. She was still wearing the splattered smock she put on when she painted in her cellar studio. After digging in the tangled heap in the drawer a while, her mother pulled out the nightgown. "It's such a mess. No wonder you couldn't find it," she said. "But why are you packing? I thought it was Claire's turn to spend the night here."

"She didn't want to." Alice frowned, but only for a brief minute. "Claire said she'd rather spend the night at home." Alice looked up at her mother. "It doesn't matter, Mom," she said brightly. "It's really one big house."

"Oh, how is that?"

Alice pulled her mother to the window. "See?" She pointed to the hedge between the houses. There was the familiar opening made out of all their comings and goings.

"Claire's house is really my house and my house is really Claire's. It's one big house and the hole in the hedge is the door from one part to the other," she said.

Her mother smiled. "Well, I never thought of it that way."

"I can even see into Claire's room from the top of my bunk bed."

"Can you really?" Her mother laughed. "I didn't know that."

"Yes," said Alice. "I know every inch of Claire's house just like ours."

"Well, it doesn't surprise me," said her mother. "Run along, now, and have a good time."

Alice slammed shut her suitcase, kissed her mother good-bye, and dashed outside. She scrambled through the opening in the hedge and straight into Claire's house. Since kindergarten they hadn't

knocked or rung a bell. Alice smiled. When you lived in the same house there was no need.

"Claire!" she called, standing in the kitchen, "I'm here!"

Now it was bedtime. They had had supper and played three games of checkers. Then they had practiced doing the three-legged race up and down the street several times. They had practiced for the last few days. Claire's birthday party was soon, and Alice wanted to be sure the two of them would win first place.

Alice lay in the bed next to Claire. "I bet I can find the bathroom with my eyes closed," she said suddenly in the darkness.

Claire giggled. "I bet you can't," she answered.

Alice knew Claire was only playing the game. "You know I can!" said Alice. "I'll prove it." She sat up.

"Okay, show me," said Claire in a whisper. "But be quiet. We're supposed to be asleep."

Alice began walking to the door with her thin hands outstretched in front of her.

"How do I know you aren't cheating?" whispered Claire. "Maybe you're looking."

"I am not!" said Alice, and bumped into the doorjamb. "Ouch!"

Claire giggled.

"Stop laughing," hissed Alice, and in three strides went across the landing to the bathroom. She ran back to Claire's room. "I did it," she said triumphantly. "I can go anywhere in your house with my eyes closed. Just like at mine. I feel like I live here." Alice climbed into the bed. "Isn't it fantastic? It's like we really *are* sisters, Claire. Forever and ever."

Claire was silent. Alice could hear her breathing. "Claire?"

"Yes."

"You aren't saying anything."

"I'm thinking," said Claire.

"Me too," said Alice quickly, then. It was silent for a moment. Alice could hear the ticking of the alarm clock. "What are you thinking about?" she asked finally, a little edge of impatience creeping in.

"About my birthday party next Saturday."

"Oh." Alice was disappointed. Claire wasn't thinking about being sisters. She frowned. Didn't best friends always think about the same things? Alice turned sharply in the bed. "Well, what about the birthday party?" she asked a little crossly.

"I'm just wondering, you know, thinking about the presents . . . and everything."

17

"Oh."

"I remember my party last year," said Claire. "Do you remember? Do you remember when you got punch all down the front of you?"

"Yes!" Alice giggled in spite of herself. "You spilled the whole pitcher all over me."

Claire laughed. "And you were so surprised you dropped the cake on my new shoes and the icing went *splat!*" Claire's voice broke into gales of laughter.

"There was chocolate icing on everyone's socks like brown chicken pox. It sure was a sticky party."

"You know," said Claire suddenly, "you've been to every one of my parties."

"I know," said Alice solemnly.

"Every single one!" said Claire. "In fact, you've known me since I was a baby and I've known you since you were a baby."

"I know," said Alice softly.

"I bet we'll know each other our whole lives," said Claire, testing out the idea. Her voice sounded tired and distant.

"Yes," said Alice, and snuggled into bed. She didn't want to hear Claire's funny new voice. Just then she wanted to feel warm and special.

"We'll know everything about each other, Claire.
Oh, let's be best friends forever and ever." She
said it lovingly.

But Claire didn't answer.

"Claire?"

Silence.

"Claire?"

Even though Alice hadn't wanted to hear it, Claire's voice *had* sounded funny. Maybe it was because Claire was sleepy. That had to be it! There wasn't a sound in the room. Alice smiled in the dark. Claire was asleep. That explained everything. Alice sighed and curled up tighter in the bed.

"Forever and ever," she said then to herself.

❧ *Chapter Three* ❧

Alice went to Claire's birthday party early. It was a cold March day. She wiggled through the opening in the hedge, holding Claire's presents. She had spent a long time selecting the presents. They were all things she wanted herself, and she couldn't wait another minute for Claire to open them.

"Hello!" Alice yelled, and walked straight into the house. "Claire! I'm here!"

"Alice?" Claire ran to the kitchen. She was wearing a pink party dress. Her eyes were wide with excitement under the mop of blond hair. "Hi!" she said and eyed the presents.

"Here. Happy birthday!" said Alice, spilling the presents on the kitchen table. "Open them!"

"Right now?"

"Yes, before the others come," said Alice.

Claire flushed and looked at the clock. "I should really wait. The party isn't until three."

"No." Alice stamped her foot. "I brought them early . . . on purpose," she said determinedly.

Claire looked at Alice and then at the presents. "You're always telling me what to do," she mumbled, and put her hands behind her back. "All the time, Alice."

Alice looked up, surprised. "You don't have to," she said, a little hurt. "It's just . . . well, that I can't wait. . . ."

Claire balanced on the balls of her feet. "All right," she said at last. Slowly, deliberately she undid the wrappings.

"Hurry!" said Alice.

Claire opened each package carefully. "Oh, an elephant poster. Alice, it's beautiful. And a whole bag of cat's-eye marbles . . . and a stuffed . . . stuffed mouse."

"I made it," said Alice, grinning. "All by myself."

"Oh, I love them all," said Claire. She took a skip into the kitchen. "You've always given me the best presents."

Alice sighed and nodded. Yes, they were the best presents. She knew it. She wanted to be the one to give Claire the best presents of all.

A little later the doorbell rang. The others were coming.

"Don't forget we do the three-legged race together," said Alice before Claire went to the door.

Claire nodded. Alice smiled with satisfaction. They would win that race. Alice was sure of it.

Slowly, one by one, the other girls came. All of them had presents. Alice watched Claire carefully. She could tell Claire liked the others' presents, but even so she knew she had brought the *best* presents of all.

The last to arrive was Jessica. She brought a strange, squeaky present in a square box. Everyone stopped what they were doing and watched Claire open it. Her hands were trembling.

"What is it?" she said. Her voice went higher and higher. "What is it? Oh, Jessica, what did you bring?"

Alice felt suddenly cold. She saw the paper drop away and there was a guinea pig in a cage.

"Oh, look!" Claire stood speechless. "Oh, Jessica, a guinea pig. How did you know I wanted one?" Claire stuck her hand in the cage and seized the guinea pig. Everyone crowded around. Everyone but Alice.

"Isn't he cute?" Claire's eyes danced. "Oh, Jessica, I just love him."

"Can I hold him?" asked Marie.

"Let me!" said Susan.

"No, it's my turn," yelled Fran.

They were all crowding in around Claire. From a distance Alice watched the others. She felt removed, as if she were looking at them from far away.

"Stop pushing. Nobody, nobody at all is going to hold him," said Claire suddenly, and held the guinea pig above her head. She pushed her way through the girls and Alice could see Claire's lip tremble and her eyes fill up. Claire was going to be teary.

I don't care, she thought, but from the corner of her eye Alice watched Claire curl up in the rocker with her guinea pig.

And there Claire stayed. The party went on all around her, but Claire didn't move. Her mother even had to bring the cake to her so Claire could blow the candles out.

After refreshments came the games. Alice won second at the potato race, and Marie won first in the sack race. When it was time for the three-legged race, Alice waited for Claire to come, but she didn't move out of the rocker.

"Claire!" called Alice, "it's time. It's the three-legged race."

"I don't want to," said Claire, and didn't even look up.

Alice stared. "But we practiced . . ." she began to say. "We. . . ." Right then she wanted to stamp her foot and yell CLAIRE!!! so loudly her friend would jump a mile high.

Already the others had begun the race. Alice

could hear the laughing and squealing in the long hallway. She made her hands into fists and went over to Claire.

Her friend was bent over the guinea pig, holding him tenderly. She didn't look up at Alice.

"He's so cute," murmured Claire. "Isn't he?"

"Mmmmmmm," said Alice. Some of the anger slipped away. The guinea pig was adorable.

"I could hold him forever," said Claire.

Alice gazed at the guinea pig. Then she looked at Claire. Even if they hadn't done the three-legged race, at least Claire could let her hold the guinea pig a little while.

Alice stretched out her hand. "Let me," she said.

Claire looked up. "No, Alice," she said, and shook her yellow curls. "Not now. Maybe later."

Alice blinked. She didn't understand. She didn't know whether to cry or to punch Claire in the stomach. She wanted to do both, but instead she whirled on her feet.

"I'm going home!" she yelled fiercely. Then she ran out the front door, letting it slam with a loud bang behind her.

⤳ *Chapter Four* ⤲

Things did not get any better. Claire seemed completely wrapped up in Sam, her guinea pig. She was like that day in and day out. Alice didn't know what to do. She felt upset and miserable. When she tried to be interested in the guinea pig, Claire would not even let her hold him. In the days after the party, it seemed to Alice she had touched Sam only once.

Alice began to stay at home. There wasn't any point in asking if Claire wanted to play. She was playing with the stupid guinea pig, which Alice could well see through the window. From her top bunk she could look straight into Claire's room.

The spring weather was raw and cold. It wasn't good for playing outside. And then Thursday came, when Claire went to her ballet lessons.

Alice could see Claire leaving with her mother. She watched the car pull out. Suddenly Alice wanted to go over and see Sam—just look at him and try . . . try to understand.

Alice slipped out and ran up to Claire's room. She stood in the doorway. The room felt different, as if . . . as if it had changed, grown separate, somehow, and strange. Alice had no place in it anymore.

She hesitated. Then she walked in, going over to the cage where Sam was squealing. He was a cute guinea pig with white and brown fur. But Alice didn't like him. She stared at him a long time. The more she looked, the more she hated him.

Suddenly she knew what she wanted to do. She'd take Sam and hide him. Not steal him, just hide him for a day and see how Claire felt then. Alice nodded to herself. She'd show Claire how it felt to . . . to . . . Alice shivered. Quickly she reassured herself that she'd only hide him for a day, until Claire understood, came to her senses.

Swiftly Alice picked up the cage. She darted back through the hedge to her own house. Nobody saw her. Nobody would know about Sam. She knew her mother was in the cellar, painting, and

that she wouldn't come up for some time yet.

Alice drew a deep breath once she got to her own room. She looked around and knew immediately that she could not keep Sam there. If Claire came, that would be the first place she'd look. Where could she hide him?

The garage! Why hadn't she thought of it? Alice picked up the cage and flew to the garage. Sam would be safe there in a corner. Alice made a warm nest for Sam, sheltering the cage with canvas and old burlap bags. All the time her heart banged loudly. She double-checked that Sam had everything he needed, and then she went home to wait for Claire to come back.

It was a long wait. Alice looked out the window every few minutes. At last she heard the car wheels on the gravel. Alice held her breath. One minute went by. Alice breathed shallowly. Five minutes went by.

The phone rang. It would be Claire. Alice smiled. It was the first time since before the birthday party that Claire had called.

"Hello?" Alice answered.

"Alice. Sam's gone!" said Claire breathlessly. Alice could hear the tears bunching up behind Claire's nose. "Did you take him?"

"No," said Alice. Her own voice sounded strangely cold and determined.

"But who else would?"

"It wasn't me," said Alice, and hung up.

A few minutes later the phone rang again. Claire's mother called and wanted to speak to Alice's mother. They talked a long while.

Alice tried not to listen. She dug in the cupboard for some crackers. She read the comics in the paper. Then, at last, her mother hung up.

"Alice," she said and turned. "Alice, are you telling the truth about Sam?" Her mother looked long and hard at her.

And Alice looked straight back at her mother.

"Yes," she said without blinking, without swallowing. But inside her stomach grumbled. There was a funny hollow place under her rib cage. She was afraid.

That night Alice went to bed early. But she didn't fall asleep right away. Even after the light under her parents' bedroom door was out, she was still awake.

When she woke up the day was gray. Alice looked out the window. It looked cold. She listened to the house. Nobody was awake. The pipes were hissing with steam. Slowly Alice crawled out of bed. She knew it must have turned cold for the heat to come on like that.

Then softly, quietly she slipped down the stairs and to the kitchen door. The icy wind almost tore the door from her hand. It was so cold she gulped. Now she was worried about Sam!

She ran to the garage, glad she had thought of the burlap bags and the canvas to keep Sam warm.

But when she lifted the canvas away, she knew something was wrong. Sam was on his side looking . . . looking skinny and stiff. Alice put her finger between the bars and touched him. He didn't move. He was cold and dead.

≽ *Chapter Five* ≼

Alice stood very still. The icy wind whipped through her pajamas. She didn't know what to do. She only wished she were dead too. She stared and stared at the cage until she turned blue with cold.

What could she do? Whatever could she do? She knew she had to go back to the house sometime. Slowly she turned. Slowly she made her way back to the house, back into her bed. It seemed ages before her mother came to wake her for school.

"Time to get up, darling!" Her mother's voice was cheerful. It jangled against Alice's ear.

"I can't, Mom," Alice mumbled. She burrowed her face in the pillow. "I don't feel well."

Her mother brought the thermometer.

"It's not a fever. It's a stomachache," whis-

pered Alice. She didn't look at her mother, didn't touch the tea and toast her mother brought a little later. She could only think about Claire and the way Sam looked now in the cage.

Then, before Claire left for school, she came over. Alice saw her coming, through the window.

35

Across the drive, through the hedge. Claire's face was all blotchy and Alice knew right away that Claire must have been crying all night.

A cold dread welled up inside Alice. She swallowed and crawled deep under the covers. What could she say to Claire now? She hunkered down further. If only Claire wouldn't come.

A few minutes later the door opened. Alice could feel her mother's eyes, could hear Claire crowding in at the door.

"Alice seems to be sleeping," said her mother. "Come after school, why don't you, Claire?"

Claire mumbled something back and then the door closed. Alice lay in the blackness of the bed-clothes and sweated. She felt herself spin in the dark. She wished she would never have to come out from beneath the sheets. Never!

After school Claire didn't come. She called instead. Because the doors were open Alice could hear her mother answer the phone, could hear her say, "Oh, Claire. No. I'm sorry . . . Alice is about the same. Maybe tomorrow she can see you. Good-bye." There was the click of the receiver.

Time crawled by slowly, slowly. At supper she didn't eat anything. She turned her head to the wall instead. Late in the evening her mother came in and gave her a get-well card Claire had made and brought over. Alice took it, but she couldn't look at it. When her mother left, she thrust it under the mattress. But all through the night she knew it was there—could almost feel it burning its way to her through the mattress.

❧ *Chapter Six* ❧

Alice woke up very early. Her mouth was dry and felt papery, like a milkweed pod with the seeds all gone. She sat up and felt a little dizzy. Slowly she looked out the window. Her mother had forgotten to pull the blinds. It was a sunny day. Alice gazed across the way—straight into Claire's room. Claire couldn't see her, but from the top bunk Alice could look down into Claire's room.

Claire was sitting up in bed too, just staring. And suddenly Alice knew what she must do. She had to tell Claire about Sam—no matter what would happen.

Quick, quick before she could change her mind, she got dressed. Her thin hands fumbled with the buttons and her legs felt wobbly. She managed to put a few things on. That was good enough. Silently she opened the door. Silently she tiptoed down the stairs and ran out the back door.

Claire's house was quiet. She closed the kitchen door softly behind her. No one was up. Like a shadow she stole up to Claire's room and knocked.

"Claire?"

Claire came to the door in her pajamas. Her hair was all rumpled. She looked sleepy and then her eyes widened.

"Alice!" She pulled Alice into her room. "Are you all right?"

Alice stared at Claire. She swallowed hard. "Claire . . . Claire, I've got to tell you something. I killed Sam."

Claire sucked in her breath with a little gasp and stared at Alice.

"Honest, I didn't mean to. I feel so awful." The words tumbled out. She didn't dare breathe or stop talking. "You wouldn't play with me. You've been acting funny a long time, like you don't want to be best friends. And when you got Sam, you only played with him. You didn't care about me anymore. So I thought I'd just take Sam for a little while to teach you a lesson." She gulped down some air. "And . . . and I put him in the garage.

I thought he'd be all right, honest. I put burlap sacks and canvas around his cage for warmth and I gave him water and everything . . . and then, he still died in the night. He's in the garage. It was too cold for him, and, Claire, I'm sorry. I didn't mean. . . ."

Claire just looked at Alice. Her blue eyes grew wider and wider. But she didn't say anything, not one word. Her tongue ran over her lips and she just stared.

Alice felt frozen. The cold went all the way to her toes. Always before, Claire would cry when she was upset, but now she just stared. Alice stood there swallowing, looking at her friend. Then suddenly, because she couldn't stand it anymore, she turned.

"Bye, Claire," she mumbled, and grabbed for the door. She ran all the way home. Why? Why did Sam have to die? Why had she taken him? Why?

Alice burst into her room. Now she knew that she and Claire would never be friends again.

≥ *Chapter Seven* ≤

The phone in her parents' bedroom rang. Alice could hear her mother answer. She knew it was Claire's mother calling. Because the doors were closed the words were muffled. Alice couldn't hear clearly. She fidgeted, pulled the bureau drawers out.

Alice was waiting. She knew now that any moment her mother would come in, would look at her with disappointment and disapproval. Alice felt her skin prickle, could feel what her mother's look would be like.

But her mother didn't come. Finally Alice opened the door. Her mother was still on the phone. Alice heard her say to Claire's mother, "I think you're right. The girls will have to settle it their own way."

Alice shut the door quickly then. Her mother didn't know, but it was already settled, settled for good. Alice banged all the bureau drawers shut. She pulled down the blinds and sat like a lump by the desk.

All morning her mother didn't come in. Finally, around noon, Alice heard a noise on the driveway. She opened the blinds to look. There was Claire going to the garage. Alice watched. Soon Claire came out again with a shovel. Then she went toward Alice's garage.

Alice knew what Claire was going to do. She was going to get Sam and bury him. She saw Claire put the cage near the opening in the hedge, the natural door they had made just by going back and forth all these years. Then Claire started to dig. The ground wasn't very hard because the sun was shining and the frost had thawed it. When she had a big enough hole, Claire went into her house and a few moments later the phone rang.

"It's for you, Alice!" called her mother.

Slowly Alice left her room. Gingerly she held the phone. Her hands were warm and moist, and they shook a little when she took the receiver.

"Hello," she said.

"Alice?"

"Claire?"

"I'm burying Sam. You can come if you want to."

Alice swallowed. "Okay, Claire, I'll be right there."

She put down the receiver, took her coat, and went outside. Claire was waiting for her. Slowly Alice approached. She stood by the hole on her side of the hedge.

Solemnly Claire put Sam in the hole. She didn't say anything. She shoveled a little dirt on top, then more, until the hole was filled up and she had tamped it down hard with her feet.

Alice stood there and waited and then tears came all on their own. They felt strange on her face—a little cold when the wind blew.

"I'm sorry, Claire," she said at last.

Claire looked at Alice slowly. "It was my fault too," she mumbled.

They didn't say any more. They just went home, each to their own house.

In the next days, Alice and Claire went to school together and during school they gave each other the signal to meet by the water fountain. They

walked home together too, most afternoons. And sometimes Claire would invite Alice to spend the night or Alice would invite Claire to spend the night.

Each time Alice went to Claire's house, she'd cross by the opening in the hedge and each time she'd think of Sam and what happened.

So spring went and summer came. And every now and then Claire wanted to play with someone else or Alice did. It seemed harder to be friends, somehow. When she played with Claire, she had to remember to be careful not to tell Claire what to do. And sometimes playing with Claire meant . . . well, it seemed to Alice there was another hedge, a hedge in her mind, one she had to cross through. And she wondered if Claire had to cross one too. Alice thought she probably did.

They *did* cross. That was the important thing. They did cross because they were old friends . . . she and Claire.

GUNILLA B. NORRIS was born in Argentina while her father was there as a diplomat from Sweden. Her books for young people include *A Feast of Lights, Lillan, The Top Step,* and *Green and Something Else.* Mrs. Norris also spends time teaching improvisational theater and movement to children. She lives in Riverside, Connecticut, with her husband and two children.

DALE PAYSON is a graduate of Endicott Junior College in Beverly, Massachusetts. She also attended the School of Visual Arts in New York City, where she now lives. Among the books she has illustrated is *If You Listen,* which was written by Gunilla Norris. Miss Payson used soft pencil for her illustrations; she says she particularly enjoyed working on *The Friendship Hedge* because it brought back memories of her own childhood, and that she identified with Alice.

The display type is set in Bulmer and the text type is set in Caledonia. The book is printed by offset.